Hooray for Bread

THE BAKERY

Freshly Baked Bread and Cakes

OPEN

This is the tale of a loaf of bread
From the day that it was born

In a baker's oven, baking hot
On a cold and frosty morn.

This is the tale. I'll tell it now
No need to ask me twice

It's full of fun and flavor
And I'll tell it . . . slice by slice.

HOORAY FOR BREAD!

Allan Ahlberg • Bruce Ingman

CANDLEWICK PRESS

The first slice was a crust, of course
The baker ate it early
He loved its crusty crunchiness
And it made his hair all curly.

The baker's wife had the second slice
On a tray with a steamy cup
Sunlight shining in the room
And the baby waking up.

The next two slices made a pair
With butter, cheese, and ham
A sandwich for the baker's boy
And the baker's boy's dog—Sam.

HOORAY—WOOF,

WOOF—FOR BREAD!

The loaf of bread was smaller now
It sat there on the shelf
Dreaming of fields of wheat, perhaps
And humming to itself.

The next slice went out for a ride
With the baker's wife and baby
They fed the fat and feathery ducks
And a couple of fishes, maybe.

HOORAY—QUACK,

QUACK—FOR BREAD!

Then beans on toast at lunchtime
And boiled eggs for tea
With bread-and-butter soldiers
All lined up — one, two, three.

Two slices, though, I have to say
Were unaccounted for
They somehow, sort of . . . disappeared
(In time I'll tell you more).

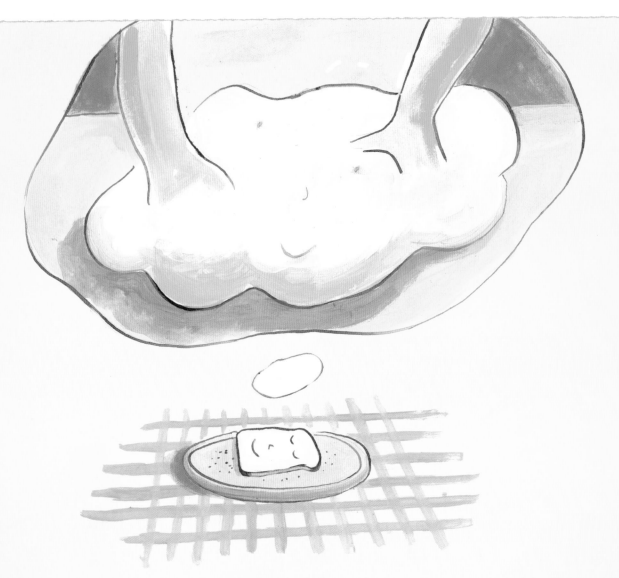

The loaf, meanwhile, was a shadow
Of the loaf we've come to know
It lay there on the breadboard
With its dreams, perhaps, of dough.

But see the tale is almost told

There's little more to come

The loaf is on its final lap

So I'll tell it . . . crumb by crumb.

The crumbs are on the breadboard
The window's open wide
The beady birds are waiting
On the garden wall outside.

HOORAY—TWEET,

TWEET—FOR BREAD!

It's bedtime in the bakery now
The family's all asleep
While elsewhere in the darkened rooms
Small creatures prowl and creep.

There's one last crumb remaining
In the silent sleeping house
And it ends up in the tummy
Of a teeny, tiny mouse.

Those missing slices, by the way
Have not gone very far
Just turn the page and you will see
Exactly where they are.

A pair of pages full of food
A tasty double-spread
For you, with these concluding words . . .

For Alvie, Ted, and Ramona
B. I.

13 14 15 16 17 18 LEO 10 9 8 7 6 5 4 3 2 1

Printed in Heshan, Guangdong, China • This book was typeset in Gill Sans. • The illustrations were done in pen and watercolor.

Candlewick Press, 99 Dover Street, Somerville, Massachusetts 02144

visit us at www.candlewick.com